Franetta McMillian

THE HOLOLOUNGE OF THE MUNDANE

Cover: *Blue Wave* by Franetta McMillian

ISBN:9798669505165

Franetta McMillian
marybld@aol.com

Shout out to: Delaware Zoom Writers, who patiently listened to early drafts, Clover, for introducing me to the backrooms, and S, who likes to be invisible.

For the plague dead and those left behind

"Love is the only way down..."

-- Lianne La Havas

One   9

Two   15

Three   20

Four   24

Five   26

Six   28

Seven   41

Eight   45

Nine   50

Ten   58

Eleven   86

Twelve   90

Thirteen   94

Fourteen   99

Fifteen   101

About the Author   114

ONE

Evelyn Barnes sat at her kitchen table doing what she did every morning: leisurely eating breakfast, having her morning scroll. She subscribed to three newspapers: the *New York Times*, the *Washington Post* and the closest thing her area had to a local rag, the *Clinton County Trawler*. The headlines in all three were uniformly bad. Cases of COVID-19R2 were spiking with no end in sight; that August was well on its way to being the hottest on record, and most places in the beleaguered country either had far too much rain or not enough.

Ms. Evie lived in a place with too much. The view outside her floor to ceiling windows looked more like the Amazon rainforest than southeastern Pennsylvania. Hot steamy green as far as the eye could see. Of course, maybe that was a good thing since the actual Amazon rainforest was in flames. If the earth decided to sprout a new set of lungs in her backyard, Ms. Evie was okay with that.

But then again, she really didn't have a choice. The landscaping company had terminated its contract with the subdivision after one of their employees was attacked by a murder hornet and perished on her next door neighbor's porch. And Ms. Evie wasn't about to go out and trim that mutant greenery herself. She freaked if she saw a baby spider in her laundry room.

So there she sat, scrolling through her email. Ho hum... The bulk of it was ads for gourmet food, prepper gear, and designer hazard wear, none of which she could afford, although she was jonesing for one of those new premium haz suits with climate control. That way she could go outside when the sun was out.

Eventually, she put down her phone and yawned. Crap. Only 8:30. She yawned again. Never once did Ms. Evie dream the end of the world would be so goddamned boring. She was dying for school to start just for something to do -- although she knew after a couple weeks with sullen, whiny tweens she'd be wishing it was summer again.

Her phone chimed. She thought it might be her friend Ms. Vicki from up the street reminding her about their virtual happy hour that evening, but instead it was an invitation from someone named Tori to something called *The Hololounge of the Mundane*. There was a link at the bottom of the text.

Though sorely tempted, Ms. Evie did not click on it right away; she wasn't that foolish. Instead, she called Ms. Vicki. "Hey Vick," she said, "you ever heard of a scam involving something called *The Hololounge of the Mundane?*"

Ms. Vicki just laughed. "Nope, I ain't heard of that one yet. What is it?"

"I don't know. That's why I called you."

"Well, you could just look it up, y'know. You forget we're all omniscient now."

Oh yeah, the magical internet machine. Ms. Evie always did forget about it when it could actually be useful.

Vicki asked: "Why do you want to know?"

"I just got a text about it. A mysterious invitation."

"Well, did you know the person who sent it?"

"Uh...no."

"Well then just delete it. It's obviously someone trying to sell you something. Or Russians trying to hack into your bank account."

Evie just laughed even though she knew her friend was dead serious. Vicki blamed any vexing online mischief on Russians or the Chinese.

"Uh, here it is," Vicki said after a long pause. "*The Hololounge of the Mundane*. It's a book that came out some 40 years ago, hailed by critics as 'the Ulysses of the 21st century'. Intellectual types loved it; real folks hated it; it went out of print in less than two months, although it did develop a cult following. The author, Tori McDonald, disappeared under mysterious circumstances. It is widely believed she was murdered…"

Evie sucked in her breath. All the memories came flooding back… "Oh, now I remember that stupid book. A professor assigned it in graduate school. Longest 200 pages I ever had to slog through, the sort of book you definitely needed some chemical assistance to understand, if you know what I mean."

"What was it about?"

"Nothing."

"Do you really mean nothing or is it that you just don't remember?"

"No, the book is literally about fricking nothing. It's basically a transcript of a virtual role-playing game where people pretend to do all the stuff they couldn't do once the plagues started. Y'know, like eating out, going to bars, having one night stands…There's no plot to speak of, just random bits of inane dialogue. And if that wasn't annoying enough, the whole thing abruptly ends in the middle of a sentence because there's a huge blackout and everyone's batteries go dead and no one can get online anymore."

"Sounds perfectly pointless," said Ms. Vicki.

"It was infuriating! I even wrote the author. *Why the hell would you torture people like this?* I swear: if it wasn't the professor's favorite book, and I didn't think it was going to be on the test, I never would have finished it."

Vicki laughed. "You mean your professor actually liked it?"

"Yeah, he loved it. Thought it was fricking brilliant and captured the mood of the times. There was even a club formed around it. Folks used to gather to read passages aloud and discuss hidden meanings."

"Sounds like one of those books people read just to prove how smart they are," Vicki said.

"Yep," Ms. Evie agreed, "and it was nothing except a load of crap."

"Hey. It also says here that part of it was thought to be written in code, that it contained the location of some buried treasure out in Arizona somewhere?"

"And also the names of the Illuminati and the meaning of life. Yeah, yeah, yeah...it was rumored to be jam packed with hidden meanings. Bulltinkie! All of it!"

They laughed. Then: silence. And in that silence Ms. Vicki could almost hear the gears turning in her friend's head and she could tell they weren't turning anywhere good. "Evie girl," she warned, "don't you dare click on that link!"

"I wasn't going to," Ms. Evie lied.

"Come on, I know you. You're bored shitless -- and I know what happens when you get bored."

"Oh come on, it'll be an adventure. And, like you said, most likely it's nothing but a convoluted sales call."

"Listen, I know all about your grand adventures."

"Hey, my last adventure got me a generous alimony payment and this house."

"It also got you nearly a decade of misery," Vicki reminded her. "Evie, just be careful."

"Okay," Evie mumbled, "I will."

But Vicki knew she wouldn't.

TWO

Actually Ms. Evie did not click on the link right away. She went down to the basement to find her copy of *The Hololounge of the Mundane*. Even though she loathed the book, she knew she still had it somewhere, probably on the dusty shelf in the corner with all her other books from graduate school.

Although she was quick to get rid of old clothing and outdated appliances, Evie almost never parted with a book, even one she didn't like. Books were sacred objects and they were meant to be read, preserved and cherished. If a book had a deadtree version, and she wanted to read it, she bought it. Somehow digital books didn't seem real. Evie had acquired a large and varied library over the years, so large that she and her ex had to finish the basement to accommodate it. She'd never had her library appraised, but several people told her she was sitting on a veritable goldmine. *I don't care*, she told them. *I don't collect as an investment or for show. I accumulate for my pleasure.*

It took nearly a half hour, but Evie finally located her copy of *Hololounge*. It was a hardback with a simple cover -- stark black background with white block text. It was still stuffed with yellow post-its from when she took notes for class. On the black flap was a picture of the author. She was a handsome Black woman in her late 20's/early 30's, dressed androgynously in a light button-down shirt and a man's tie tied in a perfect Windsor knot. Their preferred pronouns were they/them, which made their short bio awkward reading.

Evie opened to a random page. Folks were crowded in line, craning their necks to catch a glimpse of the stars walking the red carpet...

Has the lovely Cameron Lynn shown her delectable ass yet?

Not yet. They save the best for last.

U think that booty real?

Yeah, it's real to her. She paid for it.

Evie giggled. Hard to believe this was what passed for brilliant at the turn of this calamitous century. No wonder *homo sapiens* was going extinct. She opened to another page. A woman has bought a craft beer for a man she hopes to bed. They are sitting at the bar...

So what do you do?

I kill people.

LOL No, like what do you do really?

I told you. I kill people.

Oh, I get it. So...you're...a...hit man? Like for the Mafia?

Nope. I'm Army. I'm getting ready to kill some people now.

Oh really?

Yeah, I'm at work.

You're shitting me.

Nope, I'm keeping it 100%.

So like do you have your phone on a battlefield somewhere?

Nope. I'm sitting in an air-conditioned room and I'm freezing.

Is it like an office?

Kinda.

You know we're not supposed to be talking about bad stuff in here. Rule One: Keep it light.

Rule Two: Use your imagination.

This is supposed to be safe space.

No space is safe.

Dude! Are you for real?

In a way this isn't real. And it's also so real it hurts.

Listen man, it's been nice talking to you, but...

Don't leave now, honey; it's almost go time. If you want, I can share my screen.

Dude! Stop! You're freaking me out!

[Moderator]: Green Hrnt79, you are hereby banned from Hololounge. Any attempt to re-enter will be blocked.

Thanks for the save. I think he was pulling my leg, but he still gave me the creepy crawlies.

[Moderator]: No problem. Carry on and remember: keep it light.

Evie looked at what she'd written on the post-it:
*Hamfisted commentary on the endless war, the perils of
being a woman alone, even in a fantasy world*

Evie slammed the book shut and climbed the stairs. Why
was this mess of a book rearing its crazy head now? And
was the Tori who texted her really the author who'd been
vanished all these years? Well: there was only one way to
find out. First, she would do the dishes. Then she would
click that link.

THREE

And when she did, it led her to nothing except a slick website. What a disappointment! She'd been hoping for a treasure map at least.

The website didn't seem to be selling anything in particular, which was odd because whoever owned it had spent a pretty penny. A cheerful digital assistant welcomed her with her full name, spelled and pronounced correctly. Evelyn, with a long e. "Greetings, Ms. Evelyn Pennway Barnes! Thank you for your interest in *The Hololounge of the Mundane*. I'd like your permission to ask you a few questions before we can begin. May I have that please?"

Evie didn't know what to say. If these were scammers, they certainly weren't hurting for cash. The assistant's voice was state-of-the-art, nearly indistinguishable from a living, breathing human being. In fact, Evie swore she could hear breathing as the assistant awaited her response.

"I'm sorry," the assistant said patiently, "I have been rude. I haven't introduced myself. My name is Forsythia, like the flower. I'm one of the digital assistants of Tori McDonald."

"Tori McDonald is dead," Evie grumbled.

"No, they aren't," Forsythia said. "But I don't have time to explain that now."

"What do you want?"

"Your permission to ask you a few simple questions. Mr. Tori promises to keep your answers confidential."

Huh, thought Evie, *maybe that sourpuss Vicki was right. This is a scam...* "Gotcha! The Tori McDonald I'm familiar with was a woman."

"Granted, they were a woman when you last interacted, but they have since realigned."

Evie assumed Forsythia was talking about some sort of change in gender identification, but she had never heard it described that way before. "I've never met Tori McDonald," she said. "We've never...um...interacted."

"I'm sorry. I didn't mean to imply that you met them in person," Forsythia countered, "but you did write them a rather angry letter some thirty-five years ago when you were studying for your degree."

That made Evie stop in her tracks. She'd told no one about the letter. Even she'd forgotten about it until that morning. "How do you know about that?"

"Mr. Tori told me about it. It amused them greatly. It was different. You didn't tell them how brilliant they were. You saw right through the bullshit. You almost got the joke."

Evie laughed. "I knew that book was a load of crap."

"That's why Mr. Tori would like to get in touch with you. Now: may I have permission to ask you a few questions?"

Evie hesitated. The sky was steadily darkening, gearing up for yet another monsoon. A notification flashed at the top of her screen letting her know it was now officially unsafe to venture outdoors. All she had to look forward to was the sound of endless rain and rivers in the streets. Should she tell Forsythia what she wanted to know? Ah hell. Why not? If anything, it would be interesting. "You have my consent."

She heard something that sounded an awful lot like a sigh of relief. "Thank you, Ms. Barnes. Mr. Tori will be overjoyed."

"Okay?"

The questions wound up being fairly routine. Name, age, education, and type and speed of internet connection. Forsythia asked if Evie was able to participate in augmented and virtual reality. Then: "How sophisticated is your virtual hardware?"

"It's top of the line," replied Evie, somewhat proud of herself. "It's difficult enough teaching 6th and 7th grade English without the kids calling you a pixelwad because your avatar's crap and your system is out of date."

"That's good to know," Forsythia said. Then: "That's all for today, Ms. Barnes. Thank you for your responses and conversation. Mr. Tori will be contacting you soon. Do you have any questions?"

"Yeah," replied Evie. "Is that it?"

"Yes, that's all for now. Mr. Tori will eventually arrange a VR conference."

"For what?"

"I can't say," replied Forsythia. "They haven't deigned to tell me."

FOUR

"So," Ms. Vicki asked during happy hour, "what were they trying to sell you?"

"Nothing," replied Ms. Evie.

"Did they want personal information?"

"Nothing that they couldn't have gotten with a simple search."

"Huh," said Ms. Vicki. "So what was the point?"

Actually Ms. Evie wasn't sure. Her conversation (Could you even have a real conversation with a digital assistant?) with Forsythia had left her both spooked and intrigued. Whoever was behind the text and website wasn't a garden variety scammer. For one, they obviously knew plenty about her. They knew about her angry letter to Tori McDonald and exactly what it said. And Forsythia was far too advanced of a digital assistant to belong to mere amateurs.

On the other hand: she could find no current information on the whereabouts of Tori McDonald, the author of *Hololounge*. As far as the interwebs was concerned, the one hit wonder author had simply vanished into the ether decades ago. There were rumors about her being murdered, but Ms. Vicki could find no verifiable info on that, either. She would just have to wait.

"So what happens next?" Ms. Vicki asked. "Is that the end?"

"Yeah, for now," replied Ms. Evie.

"You sound disappointed."

"I am in a way. I needed something to break up all this heat, rain, and boredom. School's still three weeks out."

Ms. Vicki poured more wine into her glass. "Well I'm glad it fizzled out. That's one less thing I have to worry about."

FIVE

Two mornings later Ms. Evie's phone chimed twice during breakfast. The first text was from her principal informing her of the pre-opening in-service; the second was from *Hololounge* with a link at the bottom.

"Oh thank God!" Evie exclaimed. Outside it was pouring yet again. She clicked and Forsythia greeted her enthusiastically.

"Good morning, Ms. Barnes! How are you this fine morning?"

"Alive, safe, and bored blind."

Forsythia laughed. She sounded so natural and warm that for an instant Evie wondered if Forsythia were a flesh and blood human pretending to be a digital assistant just to mess with her. "Then I assume you should be free this evening around 7:00?"

This evening? thought Evie. Well, she had hoped for a little more notice. If this was going to be a grand adventure, she needed to mentally prepare. "Yeah, I'm free. It's not like I have anything better to do."

"Mr. Tori is very excited to meet you."

"Okay?"

"You're not excited to meet them?"

"No, I am. But I'm also confused."

"Please don't be. If you're apprehensive because Mr. Tori is a stranger, I understand, but believe me, they have no desire to harm you or your property in any way."

"Good to know," Evie mumbled.

"Just be suited up by 7. Mr. Tori will do the rest."

"Don't I need a conference room address and password?"

"No need," replied Forsythia. "Mr. Tori knows where you are."

Of course they do, thought Evie.

SIX

So, perhaps against her better judgement, at 7:00 Ms. Evie sat suited up in her conference room with her channel open. At precisely 7:01, she suddenly found herself in a bright, narrow hallway with a closed door at the end. There was even brighter light leaking out around the door's edges. *Well isn't this special,* thought Evie as she walked towards the door. *I see someone still thinks highly of themselves.*

When she reached the door, she tested the knob. The door opened easily. Then she found herself standing perilously close to the edge of a pool. The water was deep turquoise. The pool was surrounded on all sides by blindingly white walls which looked to be at least 10 feet high. The pool room had no ceiling, only a clear blue sky.

What she guessed was Tori McDonald's avatar was standing smack dab in the middle of the water wearing a bespoke three-piece business suit of all things. The turquoise water came up to about their mid-thigh.

If their avatar was anything close to reality, Tori McDonald hadn't changed much from the picture on *Hololounge's* dust jacket. The face was still clean-shaven, though slightly more masculine. The hair was shorter and graying at the temples. The Windsor knot was still tied perfectly. They appeared to be a handsome, sharply dressed man. The so called realignment had gone well. "Step in, Ms. Evie," they said. "The water's fine."

Ms. Evie had to laugh. The scene reminded her of the book: absurd and pretentious.

To her surprise, Tori McDonald laughed with her and they laughed together for a while.

Finally Ms. Evie stepped into the pool. She was wearing an avatar she often used for teaching and her skirt billowed out around her. The water was warm and soft, and came up just to her waist. The sensation was strangely pleasant. She looked at the sky. Blue as blue could be. If the walls surrounding the pool weren't so white and so high, she could imagine floating on her back in this room for hours. Still: it was an odd backdrop for a business meeting. "What is this place?" she asked.

"It's a backroom." replied Tori. "A few decades ago, this was the online gaming version of hell. You'd make a wrong move and get trapped in one of these things for hours. This is one of the more pleasant ones. Most resemble endless hallways in cheap hotels with stained carpet and cheap fluorescent lighting or abandoned parking garages. They're supposed to make you feel trapped and lost, but this one feels serene to me."

"The walls are a little too high," said Ms. Evie.

"Do you want me to lower them for you?"

"Oh no. That's not necessary."

"Really. It's no problem."

"It's a strange place for a meeting."

"I agree. But it also had the desired effect. It irked you a bit and made you laugh."

"You do relish pushing people's buttons, don't you?"

"Yes, I do," said Tori nodding. "I admit it."

"So," Ms. Evie said, "do we stand, sit, or float?"

"I prefer to float when I'm alone, but that may not be appropriate for our purposes." Tori cocked their head slightly and suddenly there were chairs.

Evie took a seat and felt like she was floating in outer space. "Christ, this feels weird!"

"Are you uncomfortable?"

Evie thought for a second. No, she wasn't exactly uncomfortable, merely weightless -- which was disorienting to say the least. Still, she shook her head.

Tori asked: "Would you like clouds?"

"Clouds?"

They gestured upwards. "Clouds," they repeated, "in the sky."

"You can do that?" Evie asked, then immediately regretted it. How stupid she must sound. Of course they could.

"Yes," Tori replied. They cocked their head again and clouds appeared.

Silence. Evie stared up at the clouds as they glided past. They looked so real, so pleasant, like the way clouds used to be before they turned capricious and dark. The hardcore gamers among her students would be impressed. "What VR system are you using?"

"An experimental proprietary quantum based system," replied Tori.

"Did you develop it?"

"Yes, the VR hardware and software are mine. The quantum computer is not. But it has opened up a host of possibilities that I'm just beginning to explore."

"I have students who would die for VR like this," Evie said. "Respect. So...is this what you do for a living? Programming? Artificial intelligence?"

"Yes," Tori replied. "Although I haven't held a regular job for quite some time now."

Silence.

"So," began Ms. Evie, "why have you brought me here?"

"First: I still owe you a response to your letter after all these years. Second: I would like you to do something for me."

"Damn," Ms. Evie said. "I'm surprised you remember that thing."

"I still have it," Tori said smiling.

"So just why did you unleash that awful book on the populace?"

"*Hololounge* grew out of my research in graduate school," Tori replied. Then, they chuckled to themselves and added, "As well as a running argument with my then future wife."

Hololounge was a bit of an accident. Tori was a doctoral candidate in Mathematics and Information Technology; their girlfriend was a doctoral candidate in English Literature. One of Tori's specialities was predictive analytics and one night during dinner they maintained they could write the next Great American Novel by algorithm, an assertion which their girlfriend, who was an aspiring novelist herself, found appalling.

"Actually she found the whole idea that complex human endeavors could be accurately described and predicted by mathematics almost sacrilegious. It left no room for the spirits," Tori explained.

"Well, I don't know about spirits, but the idea grates on me too," Evie said.

"Huh. Strange. I find it comforting," mused Tori. "Anyway: our university sponsored a competition for the best piece of book-length experimental fiction every year. The grand prize was $15,000 and publication. I bet her that if she gave me that year's theme, the judge, and a list of past winners going back ten years, I could program a novel that would be a finalist. She responded: *It's on, asshole, it's on.*"

"So you're telling me that novel was written by a computer?"

"Actually, it's a transcript of an elaborate simulation," Tori replied. "You see, when the plagues first began, there were a host of rooms that popped up online very similar to the one chronicled in *Hololounge* where people pretended to live life as if the calamities never happened. None of them were as sophisticated as the one I coded, but you get the idea. Frankly, I only expected to get on the shortlist; I never expected to win."

"You didn't cheat your girlfriend out of a prize, did you?"

"No," Tori replied. "That was the one contest she never entered; she was -- and still is -- a bit of a traditionalist. It's served her well."

"So why did you disappear?" asked Evie. "I assume you planned that."

"Fame is annoying and intrusive when it lasts longer than fifteen minutes. Plus, I was going through a very delicate time in my life. I had just begun my realignment; I'd been on hormonal therapy for less than a month when my author's portrait was taken. And I was a mathematician and a developer, not a novelist. I knew I was a fraud."

"Did you make up that bit about you getting murdered?"

"Nope. That rumor began as fan fiction. Random chaos. But I never confirmed nor denied it, so it sticks."

"So what did you do after you vanished?" asked Evie.

"I finished my degree. For twelve years I worked in international finance and earned enough for my wife and I to have a large enough nest egg so we could start a family, protect our conscience, and live our lives in peace."

"Protect our conscience?" echoed Evie. "What do you mean by that?"

"Acts of evil often begin with desperation," Tori explained. "Given the myriad negative pressures on our morals these days, I wanted to make sure those I loved were never in the position of having to sell their souls for a loaf of bread."

Well. That was logical. Although Evie wasn't sure she would have justified working in high finance that way. She asked: "What do you do now?"

"I teach, do research, freelance..."

"How many children do you have? I mean...if you don't mind my asking."

"One daughter."

Silence. Evie looked up at the clouds. One looked like a hippopotamus.

"Ms. Evie," Tori began, "I would like your help on a project of mine."

"What kind of project?"

"I am heading a trial at a veteran's hospice. As you know, since the advent of the plagues, most of us spend our last days alone, without visits from family or friends."

"There are virtual visits," Evie commented.

"True," Tori agreed, "but most of those are very poor quality."

"So you want to give the sick and dying better VR?"

"Yes, that's part of it. But I want to do more than that. These virtual environments can also be therapeutic. Take yourself as an example. When you entered my hallway, your blood pressure was borderline high and there was quite a bit of tension in your lower back. Judging from the type of tension, I'd conjecture you experience chronic back pain, most of which you chalk up to age. Now, your blood pressure reads low normal and the tension in your back muscles has dissipated. My guess is, that for once, you are not in pain."

"Because here I'm weightless?" asked Evie. She was more than a little spooked that Mr. Tori was tracking her vitals, but on the other hand, it was their world she was floating in. And they were right: she was totally pain free and she couldn't remember the last time that was true.

"There was a bit of chaos that occurred in the *Hololounge* that wasn't my doing," Tori confessed. "When the simulation ran, it appeared to outsiders as a regular private meeting room. Now, I wrote *Hololounge* to be tantalizing enough to tempt someone into hacking it, which several people tried. Only one person succeeded though. He was a drone pilot in the Army..."

Evie had a flash of recognition. "You mean that scene in the bar where the guy tells the woman he kills people for a living? That was real?"

"The guy from the Army was real. The woman who bought him the beers was not. Actually, he hacked the simulation early and mostly lurked. The bar was the only time he interacted with it. After the program booted him, he tried several times to get back in; I guess because he liked the challenge. He was finally successful at the very end, but of course, *Hololounge* disappeared not long after."

That drone pilot's name was Specialist Rupert L. Martin and he'd written Tori McDonald an angry letter too. He was pissed the private room he'd hacked and eavesdropped on to keep his sanity was just a stupid gimmick to publish a lousy book, and even more pissed the woman who may have written the code for said room was some man-hating cross-dressing lesbian. *Although I must say,* he concluded. *That was some dope code you wrote, if you wrote it. It was hard as hell to crack.*

"I've kept tabs on Mr. Martin over the years," said Tori. "He isn't doing well. His time in the military scarred him deeply, I think. He's been in and out of jail, in and out of rehab, and now he's in hospice with terminal cancer and in this trial. He has no next of kin. He wishes to spend his last days in someplace like *Hololounge*, and -- well, you know -- live a normal life. I'd like you to hang out with him."

Evie's jaw dropped. "Why me? I mean, can't a chaplain do that?"

"No," Tori replied, all too calmly, "their caseload is too heavy. They can't spare the time."

"Okay, but that doesn't answer the first question. Why me?"

"Because I think you two would be compatible."

Whatever benefit Evie had derived from being weightless quickly vanished. What exactly was Tori McDonald asking? Did they want her to chat up a strange man in a virtual bar? Maybe give him one last girlfriend experience before the Grim Reaper arrived? "What the hell?!" Evie cried, pounding her fist on the water and making quite a splash. "What did you do? Run your fancy predictive analytics on us and say, *Ding! I think I've found a match?*"

"No," replied Tori, "this is just a hunch. I haven't forgotten the value of intuition."

"Christ, you're a piece of work!" Evie folded her arms and shot Tori her best stank eye.

Silence. Then: "I'm sorry I offended you, Ms. Evie."

More silence. Then Ms Evie said: "You say this guy has no next of kin?"

"None," replied Tori.

Evie chewed on that for a bit. Suppose she were sick and dying and there was no one around to care? She didn't have any children of her own, but she could imagine her classes sending a group get well card. She could imagine Ms. Vicki with her glass of red wine chatting with her on her tablet. And she was sure some of her cousins would at least drop her a text. But if she had no one? Damn, that would suck. She got to thinking about when the first plague began, and no one was quite sure what it was, those unlucky enough to fall ill on cruise ships often died at sea. Evie thought the only thing worse than dying at sea would be dying in space. Dying with no one to care was worse than both.

"Ms. Evie," Tori said quietly, "you don't have to do anything that makes you uncomfortable. And should something about your interaction with Mr. Martin cause you to feel unsafe in any way, you'll be able to exit the simulation immediately, no questions asked."

"I'll do it," she said quietly.

"Thank you," Tori said -- and sighed as if a heavy burden had been lifted.

Then Evie asked: "You feel bad for duping this guy, don't you?"

"Yes," Tori replied, "I do. Sometimes I wish *Hololounge* had never happened."

SEVEN

"So," Ms. Vicki said, glass of rosé in hand, "I'm on pins and needles. What happened?"

"I'm still trying to figure that out." Ms. Evie had opted for something stronger that evening, a scotch on the rocks, her ex's favorite drink. On her kitchen table she had some papers that a courier had hand delivered that morning. Mostly, it was information about the clinical trial at the VA hospice she'd verbally agreed to participate in, although there was still time to back out if she wanted. There was a description of the hardware and software being tested, biographical information about her would-be partner, Rupert Martin, and a bevy of consent forms. She would have to have a physical, a psychiatric interview, and a new body map to calibrate the experimental VR gear.

There was also information about Tori McDonald's company, McDonald-Southland Virtual Technologies, Inc. Turns out the reason Ms. Evie couldn't find any current information on the whereabouts of Tori McDonald was because that wasn't the name they used professionally; instead, they went by Toren (rhymes with Lauren)

McDonald. Apparently, that had always been their legal name. Tori was a nickname.

While there wasn't a wealth of information online about Toren McDonald, there was enough. They'd spent their early childhood as a ward of the state until they attended a STEM day camp one summer and a mathematics professor at the local university discovered how brilliant they were. The professor adopted them so they could get the secondary schooling they deserved and attend university for free. McDonald published their first paper at the ripe old age of 15 and had a publication list which ran several pages. They might not have been as famous as they would have been if they had continued programming pretentious novels, but they were a luminary in their chosen field.

"Evie, you're being awfully quiet," Vicki prompted. "Spill it! I want some dirt."

Evie just laughed. "You know, for someone who was fearing for my safety just a few days ago, you're now awfully invested in this thing."

"That's because it's your job to have wacky adventures for me."

"Well, nobody was selling me anything or trying to steal my life savings," Ms. Evie began. "And it was the same person who wrote the book..."

"What did they look like?" Vicki asked excitedly.

"Look them up for yourself. Under *Toren* McDonald not, Tori. The avatar matched the person."

After a slight pause, Vicki exclaimed: "Damn, that's one fine piece of humanity right there! Got that tough pretty thing going on like a young Marlon Brando. How did you not jump that?"

"They were married. And unnerving as hell," Evie replied. "We met in a virtual swimming pool, if you can believe that. A swimming pool surrounded by gleaming 10 foot high walls that opened to a sky with clouds McDonald could control with a cock of their head. My gaming students would've been in heaven."

"So if you met in a swimming pool, did you get wet?"

"No, come to think of it, we didn't. I had the sensation of wetness, of floating, but I never actually got wet, not even in VR." Evie took a sip of scotch. "Damn, how did that happen?"

"Same as the bush that burned, but wasn't consumed," Vicki quipped.

Evie rolled her eyes. "Funny." She then told Vicki all about the clinical trial at the VA hospice, about how Toren McDonald wanted to use cutting-edge VR and AI to make the business of dying without family or friends less lonely, and how McDonald wanted Evie to partner with the vet who'd hacked the *Hololounge* simulation all those years ago.

"So this Toren dude basically wants you to be the guy's Death Angel?" asked Vicki.

"What the hell is a Death Angel?" asked Evie.

"They have them in Sweden, or Norway, or some country like that. They're like comfort girls for the dying. If you decide to off yourself, and you've got no family, they'll stay with you until you're gone."

"They just want me to talk to him. No hanky-panky involved. I can leave if I feel uncomfortable."

"You gonna do it? I mean: it ain't final until you sign on that dotted line. Think about it: even if that guy was just some drone operator sitting in an underground bunker somewhere, dropping bombs on people is still some heavy shit. He's probably got mental scars as deep as the Grand Canyon. You sure you want to deal with that?"

"Vicki, I deal with as many as 75 hormonal, confused kids who don't think they have a real future for 10 months a year. This guy doesn't scare me."

"Well, okay," said Vicki.

"Well, okay," Evie echoed, downing the rest of her scotch.

EIGHT

After she signed the papers and sent them back with the courier, Ms. Evie's life became a whirlwind of activity. For that, she was thankful. Better busy and slightly anxious than depressed and bored. For the next five days, she met with someone connected with the trial to prepare for her grand adventure. On the first day, a lab tech stopped by for blood, urine and stool samples; the next day a nurse practitioner came by to discuss her lab results and do a physical examination. On the third day she had a video interview with a psychiatrist, who asked her about her childhood, how her life had changed since the plagues, and why her marriage fell apart.

On the fourth day some techs from McDonald-Southland came by to do a body map and install upgrades to her VR hardware. For the mapping, Evie wore what she wore when she'd made her last upgrades, but apparently the body-conscious leggings and sports bra weren't body-conscious enough. "I'm sorry," the female tech said. "I'm not sure if our paperwork explained this properly, but you'll have to disrobe completely."

"Why?" Evie demanded.

"This simulation is designed to be completely immersive. Your avatar will have to function accordingly. If this makes you uncomfortable, we can make adjustments, but then we won't get a full test of the system. My partner and I can sit outside for awhile and give you space to think…"

"Uh no," Evie said quickly, before she lost her nerve. "I don't have a problem."

The techs left the room while she peeled off her clothes. When they returned, they scanned every inch of her, quickly and professionally. It was the most surreal thing she'd experienced since she had surgery on her varicose veins and her surgeon sang the Grateful Dead out of tune while she was three sheets to the wind on twilight sleep. After the scan, the techs spent until early evening installing upgrades, leaving only once to take a meal break in their van.

On the morning of the fifth day Evie got a text from *Hololounge*. Actually she got a courtesy text from *Hololounge* after every step of preparation. She and Forsythia were getting to be besties.

"Good morning, Ms. Evie!" Forsythia enthused. "How are you today?"

"I'm fine."

"Have you recovered from your tech upgrade?"

Evie shrugged. "I guess."

"Clara tells me you were a little weirded out by the mapping process. Me and Mr. Tori just want to make sure you're okay."

"I'm fine." Evie smiled to reassure her, but then felt stupid when she remembered the chat was audio only.

"So how'd you like to test your new system? Mr. Tori would like to meet you this evening at 7:00 for a test."

"They're not going to drown me in the heavenly isolation tank, are they?"

Forsythia laughed. She was getting used to Evie's droll sense of humor. "No, they aren't. The pool thing was just their idea of a joke. But while we're on that subject, do you have a specific setting you'd like to meet in?"

"On a park bench on a bright, sunny day. Nothing but cottony white clouds in the sky. And no more than 75 degrees with low humidity. Oh, and I want a stream running somewhere close."

"Any park in particular, or just a generic one?"

"I'll leave that to Mr. Tori. Let them show me what this new thing can do."

Evie swore she heard Forsythia's contented sigh. "They will be very pleased to hear that. They like showing off. See you at 7:00." Forsythia signed off.

After that, Evie's phone rang. It was Ms. Vicki, who was probably feeling a little abandoned since Evie had joined the trial. Evie switched the call to video and could see her friend was nursing a large glass of post-breakfast orange juice. Evie wondered how much vodka was in it.

"So what's with all those people in and out of your house this week?" asked Vicki.

"It's prep for the trial," Evie replied. "I had to have a physical with a full lab workup, an interview with a psychiatrist, and a body map and upgrades to my VR setup installed."

"Christ! That's a lot of strangers traipsing through your crib."

"Don't worry. They all followed protocol. I don't know what any of them look like below the eyes."

Vicki laughed. "So: you scared?"

"Yep."

"What does this new VR set up do?"

"Don't rightfully know. Me and Mr. Tori, as their digital assistant calls them, will test it out tonight."

"You met your terminal vet yet?"

"Nope, don't get to meet him until after my system passes."

"Well just be careful, girl."

"I will."

NINE

Toren McDonald delivered on the park. Precisely 30 seconds after the stroke of 7:00 Ms. Evie opened her eyes to find herself seated on a wooden green park bench on a crisp spring day facing a stream. The frogs were out in force, calling out for mates. Birds were singing. Until then, Evie hadn't realized how little birds sang in the real world. It was getting too hot even for them.

The simulation was extremely immersive, even to the point of being annoying. Ms. Evie could feel the prickliness of the aging wood on the backs of her thighs and was glad her avatar was wearing pants instead of shorts. That's all she needed: virtual splinters. And she could feel her nose begin to itch like there was pollen in the air.

"You know," Toren said, as they sat down beside her, "you can turn the pollen off."

"How?" Evie asked.

They smiled. "Just wish it and it will be so. The system is sensitive enough to read your emotion."

Evie was doubtful. "Pollen, begone!" she intoned, like a witch casting a spell. And just like that, it was gone.

"You didn't believe me, did you?" asked Toren.

"Nope."

Toren's avatar was dressed a bit more relaxed than at their first meeting. Today they were business casual with a short-sleeve peach polo shirt that displayed toned arms and crisp khaki pants with freshly ironed creases. Their medium brown skin was baby smooth, except for a slight scar on their left cheek. Their light brown eyes were warm and very kind. It was weird. Evie could better read non-verbal cues in this simulation. In the pool Toren came off as arrogant, cold, and manipulative, even when they were supposedly being considerate of her needs. Questions like *Do you want me to lower the walls for you? Do you want clouds in the sky?* felt more like a cheap display of power than true hospitality. But now, Evie could see and feel it had been a healthy mixture of both. Oh, and Vicki was right: Toren McDonald was one fine looking specimen of humanity.

"Take a picture," they teased. "It'll last longer."

Evie blushed. Had she been staring that hard? "I'm sorry. It's just that this simulation is...a...bit...um, intense." Yeah, that was it. She certainly didn't want to say, *You're not the jerk I thought you were.*

"That it is," Toren concurred. "Precisely why I wanted you to get a feel for it before you met with Mr. Martin. Traditional VR, no matter how good it is, is always a couple steps removed. This is as close to the real world as you can get without being there."

"Yet, unlike the real world, it's under your control."

"Yes."

"So you can wish away pollen?"

"Precisely."

"And if I go stick my hand in that stream over there, I'll get more than the sensation of wet, I'll actually get wet?"

"Pretty damn close. You won't be able to tell the difference. There won't be that background static of unreality that's always present in traditional VR."

"Can I die in here?" asked Evie.

"I don't know. If your body dies in the real world, you'll drop out of the simulation, but I don't think it works the other way around."

"I assume you've tested this on yourself. Have you ever gotten physically injured?"

"No," Toren replied, "I haven't. But I've often gotten an emotional wallop I didn't expect. That's what you have to watch out for."

"Good to know," Evie said.

Toren stood. "Would you like to take a walk?" they asked. "You should get used to moving around in here -- although once you start, you'll find it's quite easy."

They started walking towards the stream. Evie got up and followed. She had no trouble walking; it was easier than in the real world. Still, it was hard not to get distracted. The simulation was extraordinarily detailed, from the feel of the ground beneath her feet, to the way the blades of grass tickled her toes through her sandals. And she still couldn't get over the birdsong. Everything about the park was perfect. Who would ever believe this was how the world used to be not so long ago?

Then: Evie felt something that felt an awful lot like a stray piece of spidersilk graze her shoulder. Which meant a spider was near. She screamed and stopped dead in her tracks..

Toren stopped and turned. "What's wrong?" they asked.

"There's a fucking spider in here!"

Toren had the gall to smile like they were amused. "Aren't there always spiders in the woods?"

"I suppose -- but that doesn't mean I want them near me."

"Well then," they said, "you know what to do."

Evie shut her eyes tight. "Spider, spider wherever you are," she whimpered, "please go away..." She opened her eyes. "So," she asked Toren, "is it gone?"

Toren burst out laughing.

"That's not funny!" shouted Ms. Evie.

"It's gone if you want it to be," they replied, wiping away tears. "Just trust the tech. Oh, and a word of advice: if you want to modify the simulation, you don't have to speak your wishes out loud. The tech will read you." They started walking again. Evie steeled herself and followed.

"So how long did it take you to code all this?" she asked.

"This particular environment? Not long. It's based on a real place. Pennypacker Park in Eden, Pennsylvania, around 1990. I used to hide out there often when I was a kid."

"You had to hide?" asked Evie.

"Yes. At least I felt I did. It was quiet and I could think all I wanted out here."

"When did you first realize you were a genius?"

"No one called me that until I beat Professor Larkin at four-dimensional tic-tac-toe on my first try at STEM summer camp during the summer of third grade. Up until then, I was mostly called a weirdo, a freak, and a pain in the ass."

Evie laughed. By now, they'd reached the edge of the stream. Evie knelt and dipped her hand in the water. It was cool, wet, and clear enough to see the smooth round stones at the bottom. A couple of minnows swam around her fingers. "Wow," she said. "I'm impressed."

"I'm glad it meets your approval," Toren said.

Evie searched their face for traces of a smirk, but found none. Surprisingly, they weren't being sarcastic; they were genuinely pleased as punch their creation passed muster. "So where does Mr. Rupert want to meet?" she asked.

"He'd like to take you out to dinner," replied Toren.

"So how should I dress?"

"Something nice, but comfortable. First impressions count."

"Should I be myself or just pretend?"

"Probably a mix of both. I'll give you a hint: Rupert's avatar will look like he did when he was healthy. He sees no advantage to looking like death warmed over. He seeks your compassion, not pity."

Evie nodded. "How much time does he have left?"

"I don't know precisely, but it isn't long."

"Do you think he'll die while we're together?" she asked.

"Most likely not. His vitals have to meet a minimum threshold to play his part in the simulation. We'd cancel the session if we felt he was too close to the end."

Evie noted Toren said *most likely* -- which meant they weren't iron-clad, 100%, sure. She could wind up playing Death Angel whether she wanted to or not. The psychiatrist had even asked her: *Have you ever seen someone die?*

She felt a knot form in her gut. Holy crap. This was serious.

"Ms. Evie," Toren said, "you aren't getting cold feet now, are you?"

She watched the play of water and sunlight over stones. "No," she lied.

They knelt beside her and squeezed her shoulder. "You can do this," they said firmly, as if they were stating a scientific fact. Evie prayed Toren's faith in her wasn't misplaced. They stood, then helped her up. "Come on, we should be getting back to the real world now."

57

TEN

The following Saturday, at precisely 19:00 military time, Ms. Evie found herself waiting in the crowded lobby of a virtual restaurant. She gathered it was a seafood restaurant, probably upscale, judging from the quality of the woodwork and the nautical themed decor. There was a long line to be seated. Those in line were couples mostly, all much younger, and dressed to the nines. Ms. Evie was glad she'd dressed her avatar in a stylish navy cocktail dress and opted for makeup, a statement necklace, and heels. She felt old, but at least she wasn't underdressed.

She was supposed to meet Mr. Martin in the lobby -- or maybe he was already seated at a table and waiting for her. The pre-meeting email wasn't clear or maybe Mr. Martin hadn't yet made up his mind just how he wanted his last wish fantasy to go. He was probably as apprehensive about this engagement as she was.

Ms. Evie wished she could've had a pre-date consult with Ms. Vicki over a nice glass of merlot -- it certainly would've helped her to be less anxious -- but, according to the rules, her interactions with Mr. Martin were to remain strictly confidential. If she needed to debrief, or had any questions, she was to speak to either Toren or the psychiatrist who'd done her pre-trial interview.

There was a large picture window in the lobby, and Evie could see a few small boats on the water. She just couldn't get over how real everything seemed. The couples standing in line looked and sounded like living, breathing people with distinct faces and personalities. There was even the white noise din of multiple conversations. She wondered if Toren had modeled the crowd using real people or if the tech was generating everyone on the fly. She wondered how much data the simulation used. What kind of supercomputer could process something this complex?

Then: she noticed her feet hurt. Of course. The heels. *Stop it,* she thought, and instantly got relief.

Finally, it was her turn to check in. "Welcome to Admiral Divine's," the hostess gushed. "Reservation?"

Admiral Divine's. Ms. Evie knew the place well -- or rather she knew of it. It had been closed since the first plague. And even when it was open, it was way too rich for her blood. She kept meaning to blow her income tax refund on dinner for her and a couple of friends, but then the plagues happened, and she never got a chance. "I'm here to meet Mr. Rupert Martin," said Evie. "He made a reservation for two at 7:00? My name's Evelyn Barnes."

The hostess' eyes brightened and she smiled with recognition. "Oh yes, he's waiting for you. He's in a private booth with a most spectacular water view." She grabbed two menus. "Follow me."

"Damn," Evie said under her breath, "he went all out."

The hostess smiled knowingly. "Yes, he did."

They snaked their way through guest tables and busy servers to a sunken solarium. "Watch your step," the hostess warned. The private booths were at the far end. She slid open a glass door and Evelyn stepped into the booth. Seated at the candlelit table was a fair-skinned Black man in his mid 40s with freckles on his nose, closely cropped sandy colored hair, and the most stunning pair of gray eyes Evelyn had ever seen.

"Hi Evelyn," he said shyly. He pronounced her name correctly. Evelyn, long e. That was a plus.

"Evie's fine," she told him.

He stood and pulled out the chair for her. Evie took a seat. The hostess silently placed the menus on the table and left, quietly closing the door behind her.

"Admiral Divine's, private booth on the water..." said Evie. "Man, you went all out, Mr. Martin."

"Ru," he said.

"Ru," repeated Evie.

"This is something else," said Ru, scanning the scene.

"Yeah, it is," Evie agreed.

"I mean, this is a fricking technical miracle. I've never seen VR this good. This is better than science fiction."

"My students would die if they saw this," Evie said.

"So, you're a teacher?"

"Yeah, I teach middle school English. 6th and 7th grade."

"I sucked at English. Math was my thing. Math and computers. Actually, I sucked at middle school in general."

"Everyone sucks at middle school," Evie said. "It's an awkward age. In fact, no one could pay me to go through middle and high school again."

Ru laughed. Then silence. Then: "Would you like a glass of wine? I wonder what wine in VR would taste like."

"Sure," said Evie. "Might as well put this program through its paces."

"Notice how we're talking as if we know we're in a simulation," Ru observed.

"Yeah, I was noticing that. We're breaking one of the cardinal rules of *Hololounge* from the start. We're breaking character."

"Well hell," Ru declared, "I'm gonna die soon. I ain't got time for bullshit. All I wanted was a nice evening out, even if it was pretend."

He reached under the table for something. Apparently, there was a button somewhere to summon a server, and one appeared in short order. She was a perky coed with milky pale skin, freckles, and fiery red hair. She slid open the door. "Greetings Mr. Martin and Ms. Barnes," she announced with a million dollar smile. "Welcome to Admiral Divine's. I'm Forsythia and I'll be your server tonight."

"Forsythia," asked Evie, "are you the same Forsythia I've been talking to?"

"Why yes, Ms. Barnes," Forsythia replied. "This is my part-time gig. And I'm here to take extra special care of you two tonight. May I start you off with drinks and appetizers? The sky's the limit."

"I'll just have a beer," said Ru. "Bartender's choice. Send me something interesting."

Forsythia smiled. "Will do. And you, Ms. Barnes? What's your pleasure?"

"A nice merlot," Evie replied.

"Your wish is my command," said Forsythia with a slight bow. "Oh, and how could I forget: we also offer several varieties of cannabis for your enjoyment."

"No thanks for me," Evie said, shaking her head. "I haven't touched the stuff since college."

Ru smiled. "I'd like some...if Ms. Evie doesn't mind."

"I don't," Evie said.

"As before, your choice," Ru said. "Just not something that makes me too stupid."

"Okay," Forsythia said. "I think we can do that. And what about appetizers?"

"Fried clams," said Evie.

Ru laughed. "That's kind of lowbrow for Admiral Divine's."

"I haven't had them since I was a kid and I'm feeling nostalgic."

Forsythia smiled warmly. "And I think I know precisely the dish you're thinking of... And you, Mr. Martin?"

"Same as Ms. Evie. I'm feeling nostalgic too."

"Fine," Forsythia said, nodding. "I'll be back with your drinks shortly."

As soon as Forsythia was out of earshot (Could a digital artifact have an earshot?) Ms. Evie said, "Somehow I hadn't pictured her as a comely Irish lass."

"You've spoken to her before?" asked Ru.

"Yeah, she's one of Toren's digital assistants. She calls them Mr. Tori, though."

"Then, she's probably one of his -- I mean *their* -- older creations. Either that or she's his -- I mean *their* -- favorite. Their wife calls her Tori."

Evie giggled. "My, your pronouns are just all over the place, aren't they?"

Ru laughed. "Forgive me. I'm just a simple farm boy from Iowa. I'm learning, though. You, on the other hand, seem to have mastered the trick."

"That's because I teach -- and deal with all sorts of people and their kids. After you have a few barracuda moms call and read you the riot act about pronoun slippage, you learn real quick."

As promised, Forsythia returned with their drinks.

Ru gawked at his beer in disbelief. It was pale pink and luminescent. "Huh," he said. "Maybe I should have given her a specific brand. I can't begin to imagine what this is gonna taste like."

Evie grinned, then sipped her merlot -- and was immediately stunned. The taste, the bouquet, the sensation on her tongue. It was indistinguishable from wine in the real world.

"So how is it?" Ru asked expectantly.

Evie paused to wipe a tear from her eye. Yep, she was that blown away . "It's...perfect. And it tastes far better than anything I could afford in real life."

Meanwhile, Ru was still eyeing his beer suspiciously.

"Well? Aren't you going to try yours?" Evie teased.

"Uh...I don't know. Suppose it's radioactive?"

"Well, if it's any consolation: according to the comics, radioactive stuff glows green. That's pink."

"I swear you're not making this any easier." Ru took a deep breath, then downed a quick swallow before he could change his mind. Then: "Oh my God! Whoa, this is weird. But good. I taste a hint of strawberry, and then...there's something I can't describe... it's...like...*glow*..."

Evie rolled her eyes. "And what the hell is *glow*?"

"Here," Ru said, sliding the mug her way, "have a taste."

"I hate beer," Evie objected, pulling a face.

"This is more than beer; it's an...experience."

Evie hazarded a swallow. First: there was that nasty beer taste with annoyingly tart strawberry accents, and then...something that could only be described as...*glow*. It wasn't so much a taste as a sensation, like a flower unfurling petal by petal in your mouth, soft light, and subtle heat, followed by...peace..contentment. "Damn," Evie sighed as all her pent-up anxiety dissipated. Maybe that's why the tech had whipped it up. It knew Ru was nervous.

"I know, right?" said Ru, as he slid the mug back his way. "It's like nirvana in a beer."

Evie laughed. Although she didn't believe in auras, she swore she could feel hers glowing. "And you're gonna have a joint on top of that?"

Ru considered it. "Yeah, you're right. I should nix the pot. That's just overkill." He closed his eyes and whispered something too soft for Evie to hear.

"What did you just do?" asked Evie.

"I undid the pot," replied Ru. "We'll still get your salty, greasy, rubbery fried trip down memory lane, though."

"Thank you," Evie said.

"I aim to please...Tell you what: for our entrée and dessert, let's ask for chef's choice. No telling what we might get then."

"Well, you're welcome to do that," Evie said, "but since I'm at Admiral Divine's, I'm going to have one of those curried crab cakes smothered in that secret sauce they were known for. And then, I'm going to top that off with some of their orange zest dark chocolate cake."

Ru's eyes flashed with recognition. "Oh yeah, I remember hearing about those. Those crab cakes were like 99.9% premium crab meat with barely any filler. And didn't a slice of that cake have like a bajillion calories?"

"Yeah," said Evie. "And if you got a glass of wine, two crabcakes, a salad, and a slice of cake, it cost almost half your paycheck."

"Hell," said Ru, "it cost *all* of mine."

They laughed.

"Okay, Ms. Evie, you've gotten me good and hungry. Curried crabcakes and orange chocolate cake it is!"

That's when Forsythia appeared with their fried clams. After serving them, she asked Mr. Martin: "So how was your beer?"

"Interesting," Ru replied.

"Did you not like it?"

"Oh yeah, I liked it. It was just a bit...unusual."

"We like to experiment at Admiral Divine's. It keeps both our guests and our culinary alchemists engaged."

Evie giggled. She thought the phrase *culinary alchemists* was ridiculous. But hadn't that been what the real Admiral Divine's called their kitchen and brewery teams? She couldn't remember.

"Have you decided on entrées?" asked Forsythia.

"Yes," replied Ru enthusiastically. "And dessert too."

After Forsythia took their orders and left, Ru cleared his throat and announced: "If you don't mind, I'd like to ask you a question. Don't worry. If it offends you, you don't have to answer."

"Well with that preamble," Evie said, "you've got me scared. Out with it."

"How true is your avatar? I mean: does it look like the real you?"

"Yeah, I suppose. I don't usually wear a dress, makeup, heels, and big jewelry, but yeah, this is me. You notice I didn't bother to delete the gray in my hair."

Ru looked at her and smiled. "I don't mind gray hair. The way I figure, you live long enough, you earn it."

Evie chuckled. "I guess that's one way of looking at it. How true is your avatar?"

"It looks like I did when I was reasonably healthy, except I deleted an angry scar under my left eye I got in a fight."

"May I see it?" asked Evie.

"See what?"

"The scar."

At first Ru demurred, but then he closed his eyes, whispered something, and the scar appeared: a long, jagged raised red line just over his cheekbone.

"Damn!" Evie exclaimed. "Somebody must've hit you hard enough to crack your eye socket."

"Yeah, it's a wonder I'm not blind in that eye."

"I hope whoever hit you went to jail."

"Actually," Ru said with a self-deprecating laugh, "we both did."

"Huh," said Evie shrugging, "I can't say you look like a violent man."

"I wasn't normally. But we had all gotten buggy by then. Two years underground will do that to you."

"The fight happened when you were in the Army?"

"Yeah," said Ru, staring at his empty appetizer plate.

Silence. Evie sensed she'd crossed a line.

"I'm sorry," she said softly. "I mean, if you don't want to talk about it..."

"No...I mean, really...it's okay." Instinctively, Ru reached for her hand and squeezed it...then immediately blushed several shades of red. He'd only meant to reassure her he wasn't offended, but... "I'm sorry, Ms. Evie. I'm not supposed to touch you without expressly asking your permission."

Evie squeezed back and smiled. "It's fine. I'm giving you the okay now."

"You know," Ru mused, "this is the first time I've touched a stranger without gloves on in like...a billion years. Are your hands really that soft?"

Evie blushed despite herself. "You must've been a hit with the ladies."

"No," Ru said laughing, "I sucked at love as badly as I sucked at middle school."

He withdrew his hand and Evie noticed hers felt cold. It had been a long time since she'd touched someone skin to skin too. Not that she had really touched Ru. This was all supposed to be fake, a highly immersive dream. But that's not how it felt. *Watch out for emotional wallops,* Toren had warned. She took a breath to recalibrate.

Luckily, that's when Forsythia and another server appeared with their entrées. Ru and Evie had ordered two crabcakes each, but they were aghast at how huge they were. "I don't know why the hell I ordered two," Ru said. "These things are the size of Monsterburgers."

"Oh yeah," Evie said laughing, "Monsterburgers. I remember them."

"Well, I'll just wish this down to size," Ru said, then closed his eyes briefly. He reminded Evie of a little boy making a wish before he blew out the candles on his birthday cake. Evie nixed her extra crabcake too.

"Now this should be interesting," Ru mused as he picked up his fork. "No one ever got the recipe for Admiral Divine's secret seafood curry sauce or their crabcakes, though it wasn't from lack of trying."

"Doesn't matter to me," Evie said, digging in. "I never got to taste the real thing. I couldn't afford it." She took a bite. "Damn! This is fucking amazing!"

Ru followed her lead. "Oh yeah...hard to believe this isn't real."

"So have you ever met Toren outside of VR?" asked Evie.

"Yeah," replied Ru. "He stopped by the hospice a few times. Of course they wore hazard gear, so I have no clue what he really looks like. But from looking at their few photos online, I'd say their avatar was pretty true."

"Did you really call them a man-hating cross-dressing lesbian?" asked Evie.

"Unfortunately, I did," replied Ru. "I ain't proud of it for sure. But when I stumbled upon *Hololounge* the book, I wasn't exactly in a good place. It kicked up a lot of shit for me."

"Like what?" asked Evie.

"I found a stack of used copies at the university bookstore," Ru began. "This was a couple years after the book's initial heyday, not too long after I got out of the Army. *Hololounge*, the chatroom, was kinda legendary in my unit."

"Why?" asked Evie, "Is that what drone pilots did for kicks? Hack inane chat rooms?"

"I was more than a drone pilot..."

"Your profile said you were a drone pilot. And that's what Toren told me."

"I don't think he knows all the rest. Most of my file is redacted because the bulk of what I did was classified. Hell, I'm sure some of my file is even classified from me."

"Oooo," Evie cooed playfully, "mysterious."

"It's not funny!" Ru snapped, suddenly angry.

Evie was at once startled, chastened, and confused. This Ru was turning out to be a veritable landmine. "I'm sorry," she said.

"No, Evie, I'm sorry. You had no idea. I know I sound like one of those wacko conspiracy people, but trust me, I did some awful shit that's officially not supposed to exist. Yes, I flew drones and dropped bombs on people. But I also did other stuff that even though it was less bloody, was far more heinous."

Evie's breath caught in her throat. Suddenly the private booth felt positively claustrophobic, even though its walls were mostly glass. Evie found herself not knowing where to look, because at that moment, she was afraid to look Ru in the eye. So she stared out the window. The water was reassuringly calm. The sun was just beginning to set. Well, it's not like Vicki hadn't warned her. *Scars as deep as the Grand Canyon*, she had said.

"Evie?" Ru asked. "Are you okay?"

Evie made herself look at him. Those fabulous gray eyes of his looked on the edge of tears. This night might be his last best chance for some fun and she knew he didn't want to screw it up. She didn't either. "I'm okay," she finally said. "But may I ask one question?"

"Sure," he replied with a strained smile. "What is it?"

"Why did you hack *Hololounge*?"

"I was ordered to."

Evie couldn't believe her ears. "What?"

"*Hololounge* looked really suspicious. Supposedly, it was this silly chatboard where folks got together to pretend to do things they couldn't do once the plagues started, but it had this really top-notch security. I mean, I busted my balls trying to get into that thing, while I could hack into other places like it with my eyes closed. My superiors figured there was far more to *Hololounge* than it seemed, that it had to be some super secret terrorist hangout where people spoke in code, or a conduit for a drug cartel. So I busted my way in and listened, and discovered it was a whole lot of fluffy nothing. Which was comforting in a way, because I knew the country was a total shitshow outside that bunker."

"Yep," Evie agreed, as she recalled the first plague, "it was. Not that it's all that great now."

"I really didn't understand how bad it was until I emerged from the bunker three years later," Ru said. "Once the plagues started, they didn't let us leave until they thought the situation was under control. We were too valuable to risk losing, they said."

"So wait," Evie said, "you mean to tell me you were literally underground for three years?"

"Three years, six months, five days total."

"How did you speak to your family?" Evie asked.

"You were allowed one email a week," Ru replied. "No video chats."

"Why?"

"Chats were deemed a security risk. Folks could guess where you were even if you used a fake background -- at least that's what my superiors claimed. It made no sense to me, but I wasn't about to risk getting in trouble and getting thrown out."

Evie shook her head in disbelief. "That's insane."

"That it was," Ru concurred. "And it was all one big, fat lie."

"How so?" Evie asked.

"After a certain point, the weekly emails from my family were fake," Ru explained. "I didn't realize it at the time, because they were really good fakes -- *deep* fakes, if you will. They sounded realistic. My father lost his job and struggled for a while until he found something that paid less and was far more dangerous. My mother tested positive for the virus and had to be in isolation for a month. My sister's classes at the university would start and stop depending on how many adjuncts fell ill. The picture they painted was far from rosy, but I took comfort in their sheer determination and survival, which made the forced separation easier for me. Although after a while, it wasn't easy for any of us, even the officers."

Evie was stunned. She'd seen movies with plot lines like this, but she didn't think people had it in them to really attempt such lurid deception in real life. Obviously, she was naive. "So how did you discover the emails were fake?" she asked gingerly.

"I didn't find out until I was discharged," Ru replied. "I had this big debrief. The process took a month. They told me about all sorts of things I didn't know, that none of us near the bottom of the food chain knew. Like how near the end of the first wave, a group of angry combat vets launched a bunch of plague-ridden cadavers onto the White House lawn to protest the administration's awful treatment of vets who fell ill."

"Oh yeah," Evie said. "I remember that. Disgusting, but appropriate. I appreciated the dark humor. None of them lived to brag about it though, as they were shot long before they used all their ordnance."

Ru continued: "That's when they told me I had no immediate family left. I was so pissed, it took four people to keep me from bashing that psychiatrist's face in. And you can see me, I'm not exactly a big guy."

Evie's eyes welled up with tears. "Oh God, I can't begin to imagine!" She noticed Ru was crying too. "How did they justify that? Did they even deign to give you a reason?"

"The road to hell is paved with good intentions," Ru tearfully replied, trying to force a smile. "They told me the deception was to protect me. They wouldn't grant me leave to visit, because I wouldn't be allowed near my family anyway. So they made up a fantasy."

"Did they at least try to make it up to you?" asked Evie. "Not that you could ever atone for that."

"They decontaminated the family home and kept it up for me. I live in it free and clear. No mortgage, no taxes, no utilities. My disability payment isn't much, but it's far more generous than what a vet of my rank usually gets. I can live on it if I watch the bottom line -- which, unfortunately, I haven't sometimes. But you know what's the real kicker to this thing?"

Evie could only shrug. Frankly, she didn't see how Ru's plight could get any worse.

"I may have been an unwitting party to my own deception."

"How so?" asked Evie.

"When I was ordered to hack *Hololounge*, some people beyond my paygrade piggy-backed on my hard work and stole some of *Hololounge's* code, even though the chatroom, though hard to hack, was officially declared harmless. Somebody must've suspected it was a simulation. Especially after the book was published, which was about a year after the original room disappeared."

"So you think they used some of Toren's code to deep-fake emails from your folks?" Evie suggested.

"Yep, just like something related to that code is deep-faking everything around us. The timeline fits. And Ms. Evie, it wasn't just me. There were a lot of those fake emails. Every week, for at least 80 people. And these were long ass emails, too, more like letters. Much more than hi how are you. And they seemed so real. I mean, they got the voice right and everything. That's a *lot* of labor."

"Do you have any proof?" asked Evie -- although she could already guess what his answer would be.

"Yeah. Right," Ru scoffingly replied. "Dream on. Actually, I didn't put two and two together until I flipped through one of those used books in the bookstore and saw myself on page 89. I thought Tori McDonald had to be in on it, so she was the recipient of my wrath. That's why I was such a dickwad to them. I'm still not 100% certain Toren's code was used to generate the emails. I don't think I'll ever be. But it makes sense." Ru wiped his eyes, then looked forlornly at his plate. "Damn!" he swore. "Now my food is cold!"

"So's mine," noted Evie. She reached for Ru's hand, but stopped short. "Mr. Martin," she asked, "might I have permission to touch your hand?"

Ru's face softened, and he actually managed to smile a little. "Ms. Evie," he said, "that rule only applies to me."

Evie shook her head. "Nope. It's a two-way street."

"Of course," Ru replied.

Evie took Ru's hands in hers. "Thank you, Ru. Thank you for sharing that with me. I know it was difficult."

"Thank you for taking me seriously," Ru said. Then: "I'm sorry I frightened you."

"No sorrys," whispered Evie.

Silence. They gazed at each other, then glanced at their barely touched plates.

"Tell you what," Ru finally said. "I say we dry our eyes, wish these delicacies hot again, clear some room in our virtual stomachs, and have a feast."

Evie gave Ru's hands a final squeeze before letting go. She smiled. "Good idea, Mr. Martin. I'm down with that."

So that's what they did. They ate and talked about normal things. Evie talked about her students. Ru relayed some lighter tales of his time in the Army underground; it wasn't all lies, darkness, and death. After the initial rough patch, they got along famously -- although the endless wine and glow beer might've helped.

Finally they noticed the crowd in the restaurant had dwindled down to almost nothing. Forsythia bounced by, perky as ever, to check in. "Is there anything more I can get for you two?" she asked.

"Nah," Ru said, leaning back in his chair, "I think we're about done here." He looked to Evelyn. "Aren't we?"

"Yes," replied Evie. "I'm stuffed."

Ru said: "You seem to be close to shutting down for the night. Do we have to leave?"

Forsythia smiled knowingly. It was the first time she'd broken character all night. "Mr. Martin, I think you know full well the answer to that question." Then, she cleared the table and left.

"What have you got planned?" asked Evie, somewhat nervous.

"I just want to sit out on the balcony and watch the moon on the water," Ru replied.

"But there's no balcony here," Evie objected.

Ru closed his eyes, grinned, then opened them again. "There is now."

And there was. To her right, a sliding door appeared where there used to be a floor to ceiling window. She gave it a light tap and it slid open.

"After you, Ms. Evie," Ru said.

Evie was all set to step out to enjoy the view and the balmy breeze, but stopped short when she noticed the newly formed balcony seemed to be lacking a floor. "Your balcony has no floor, Mr. Martin," she informed him. "Did you wish hard enough?"

"Evie," he insisted, "it has a floor. It's just a glass one."

"Is it slippery?" she asked. "I've got heels on, you know."

"Then wish yourself some sneakers," Ru said, laughing a little bit too hard.

"I do believe you're virtually drunk," Evie said, playfully wagging a finger his way.

"Well," countered Ru, "so are you."

Evie traded her heels for sneakers and stepped onto the balcony. It was a pleasant night. Not too hot, not too cold. The view reminded her of a photo on a motivational poster, though not as kitschy. The inky water had just enough ripples in it to give the full moon's reflection a bit of character. She put both hands on the guardrail and breathed deeply. The air smelled slightly fishy, which wasn't entirely pleasant, but that was okay, it was supposed to smell that way. They were near the water after all.

Ru walked onto the balcony and stood beside her, placing his hand on the guardrail as close as it could get to hers without touching. They stood there for a long while, drinking in the silence, the lightplay on the water, and enjoying the night air. Finally, after clearing his throat a few times, and fidgeting like a 13 year old, Ru asked the question Evie had been half dreading all night. "Ms. Evie, would you mind if I kissed you?"

The trial guidelines banned full on sex, but flirting, hand holding, and kissing were allowed as long as both parties explicitly consented. Ms. Evie had thought out beforehand about what she would do if such a situation should arise -- she was inclined to draw the line at holding hands, just to set proper boundaries -- but now she wasn't so sure. For all she knew, this might be the last chance Ru had to experience some approximation of physical affection, because all of this wasn't real, was it?

Honestly, there was a point when she thought she knew, when she was keeping things straight, walking the tightrope, keeping her distance. Now she wasn't so sure. She knew the merlot wasn't real, yet she still felt tipsy. She knew the fried clams weren't real, but they still tasted like Friday night dinner at Captain Pete's when she was a kid. And those crabcakes and chocolate cake had been the bomb.

As were the times she and Ru touched, ever so briefly.

Yet Evie wasn't sure if she wanted to open the floodgates. Ru's trauma was definitely real. Those were real tears he'd cried, and equally real tears she had shed for him. How could his superiors have lied to him like that? Did they really think they were helping him?

She wondered what one of those Death Angel women would do.

"Ms. Evie," Ru was asking, "did I overstep? I'm sorry if I made you uncomfortable. We can just drop out and end this now if you want."

This is his last best chance, she thought. *I should give this to him.* She gently squeezed his hand, then turned to face him. "Go ahead," she said, "before I lose my nerve."

When their lips first met, it was laughingly awkward (*Damn*, Evie thought, *it's like junior high deja vu*) but then they found their rhythm. Ru didn't overstep; he knew when to quit. He kissed Evie just long and deep enough, then it was over.

"Thank you," he said, taking both her hands in his. "That meant a lot." Then he winced and held his stomach.

"You okay?" asked Evie.

Ru tried to smile, but he was obviously in tremendous pain. "Oh, it's nothing. The morphine's just wearing off. And I'm tired."

"Well, don't just stand there," Evie admonished him, suddenly switching to teacher mode. "Drop out. Get some rest."

His avatar faded before she finished her last sentence.

After that Evie dropped out too -- and crash landed in her dark conference room exhausted, confused, and feeling surprisingly lonely. She was no longer tipsy; she was stone cold sober, emphasis on the *cold*. She sat and stared into space until she could muster the energy to get up and pour herself a real drink.

ELEVEN

Toren's digital assistant, Forsythia, requested a follow-up video chat with Evie the next morning. Evie was glad for the call because she desperately needed to unload. Vicki had phoned earlier, while Evie was eating breakfast, wanting the scoop on her virtual date. She'd hung up when Evie flatly refused to talk about it, citing confidentiality rules.

"Oh come on," Vicki had pleaded. "Can't you at least tell me if his avatar was good looking?"

"Nope."

"What about the simulation itself?"

"It was okay..."

"Just okay?"

"I told you, Vick. My lips are sealed. Rules are rules."

"Aw hell! Where's the fun in this for me?"

"There is none," Evie replied. "I guess you'll have to find your own beta test."

"Go to hell!" Vicki exclaimed, half playfully, half not. Click. Evie knew Vicki would call back eventually. She was probably a little drunk.

Evie noticed Forsythia's avatar had changed slightly from the restaurant. She still had the pale skin, freckles, and red hair, but she'd aged herself to be in her 30s. Evie wondered if the alterations had been Forsythia's or Toren's doing. "Good morning, Ms. Barnes," Forsythia sang. "How are you today?"

"Alive, but dazed," Evie replied. "How's Mr. Martin? Is he okay?"

"He's fine..." She closed her eyes briefly, then sighed. "Well, he's doing as well as can be expected."

"I didn't make things worse, did I?" Evie asked nervously.

Forsythia smiled warmly. "Oh no! Of course not! If anything, you made things better. He slept well with less medication. That's nirvana for him."

Evie chuckled at the word nirvana, recalling the pink glow beer.

"He just overextended himself, that's all. You might not be as aware of this because you're reasonably healthy, but it takes a fair amount of physical stamina to be part of the simulation and he was changing things around a lot. He just wanted to do it all, I guess, while he had the chance.

And speaking of physical stamina, how are you holding up? Any adverse effects?"

"Physical effects, no, not really," Evie replied. "I got a little tipsy at the restaurant, but after I dropped out of VR, I sobered right up -- boom! -- which was disorienting, to say the least. There was no warning. You might want to make the transition from VR to real life smoother."

"Okay," Forsythia acknowledged, "I'll let Mr. Tori know and they can make adjustments. Anything else?"

"The simulation was...quite intense."

"That it is. It's meant to be totally immersive. I am merely lines of code and the first time I entered the system, I was nearly overwhelmed."

"Really?" Evie was surprised.

"I was written to be self-teaching, to absorb new data and learn from it, but Mr. Tori's new system nearly overstimulated me. It was difficult to process everything. Does that approximate your experience?"

"Somewhat," Evie replied. "But I was talking about emotions."

"Oh yes," Forsythia agreed. "I can imagine. Or perhaps: I can't. I process what you call emotion differently from you. Would you like to speak with the trial counselor?"

"No," Evie said. "I just need to sit and stew."

"Do you not wish to see Mr. Martin again?"

Evie thought about it and decided it would be terrible not to see the trial to its end, although she knew it was doomed to end in tears. The tech would work or it wouldn't, but Ru would die soon either way. It wouldn't be fair to Ru to quit, and to be honest, it wouldn't be fair to herself. Because Evie needed this too. Her night with Rupert Martin had given her something all her virtual happy hours with Vicki couldn't. Even teaching couldn't do it. She had a purpose now, she had meaning, she had a way outside herself all because she had touched him and it felt real. "Yes," she finally replied, "I'll see him -- if he's up to it."

"That's excellent!" said Forsythia, gleefully clapping her hands. "Mr. Martin will be very pleased. You'll be receiving a communication from him within the next two weeks. Mr. Tori and I thank you for your work on this project." She waved and signed off.

TWELVE

Evie didn't hear a peep from Ru, Forsythia, or *Hololounge* for almost three weeks. The sudden radio silence had her worried. Maybe she had screwed up and Toren via Forsythia was too nice to tell her. Maybe they'd stopped the trial because of what Ru had revealed while in the simulation. Or maybe: Ru had left this mortal coil and she didn't get a chance for a proper goodbye.

She was surprised she cared so much. Because really: she'd only met Ru once and they'd shared a few hours of high tech make-believe. There were some tears, some hand holding, and one awkward kiss. It was a first date like so many other first dates she'd had through the years. So why did his absence hurt like a physical thing? She thought about texting Forsythia for some news, but if Ru had indeed died, she wasn't ready to hear the words. Maybe she wasn't cut out for this Death Angel thing.

Thankfully school started. Ru remained on Evie's mind, but lesson plans, classes, students, and grading homework kept her head full enough that thoughts of him didn't overwhelm her.

Of course that's when she finally heard something. She was at her kitchen table hunched over her laptop reading the twentieth awkwardly written *What I Did This Summer* essay for the evening, when her phone dinged with a text from *Hololounge*. She clicked the link. Forsythia appeared on the screen, still wearing her Irish lass avatar with a few more changes. Now she wore her hair in a stylish bob.

"Hello, Ms. Evie," she said. "How are you this evening?"

"Happy for the break," Evie replied. "I'm grading essays about what my students did this summer. You can only read so much about the latest VR game."

"I take it classes have begun."

"Yep, it's been almost a week now."

"First," Forsythia began, "I must apologize for my lack of communication. We didn't forget about you. We had to make a few adjustments to the tech and…"She paused briefly and cast her eyes downward. "I'm afraid Mr. Martin hasn't been doing too well."

Evie nodded. "I thought so."

"He has wanted to see you again, but he hasn't been able to meet the physical minimums necessary for the simulation."

"So, um, what are you saying?" asked Evie, wishing Forsythia would get to the point, even if it was bad news.

"We adjusted the tech so we could honor his wishes," Forsythia replied. "Technology is worthless if it isn't adaptable. We made it possible for him to see you again. You will notice a subtle drop in intensity from last time, but at least Mr. Martin will be able to continue with the trial."

"You changed the tech just for him?"asked Evie. She was impressed.

"For him and others like him," Forsythia replied. "We hope to use this technology to help all those separated from the outside world due to illness. We also made the alterations you suggested. The transition from simulation to reality should be much more fluid, even if you exit the simulation abruptly."

"Good," Evie said. "Because the last time it was really jarring."

Forsythia smiled. "I apologize."

"So when would Mr. Martin like to meet?"

"Saturday at 7:00 in Mr. Tori's pool. Certainly you remember it."

"I do," Evie confirmed. She wondered what the pool room would feel like with the new system, even though the system wouldn't be running at maximum capacity.

"It's a pleasant environment," Forsythia added dreamingly. "Very peaceful. Mr. Martin has been spending a lot of time there lately."

Ms. Evie could guess why.

THIRTEEN

At precisely 19:00:30 that Saturday, Evie found herself walking down the same hallway where her surreal adventures in VR began. At least this time her avatar was properly dressed for the pool behind the door. She'd chosen modest swim capris paired with a short sleeve swim tee. She didn't want to show too much skin, not that her skin was all that exceptional. But she was setting boundaries, trying to keep it straight, avoiding emotional wallops where she could.

Imagine her surprise when she opened the door to see Ru's avatar standing in the turquoise water wearing almost the exact same thing.

"Hey, Ms. Evie!" he called. "Look! We're twins!"

Evie laughed. The pool room looked pretty much the same as the time she'd first met Toren there, except the walls surrounding the pool weren't as high and blindingly bright. The sky was different too. Ru had chosen an evening sky, with dramatic multi-colored clouds and a pink supermoon. And even though Forsythia had hinted about a subtle drop in quality, there was none Evie could see.

"Wow!" exclaimed Evie. "I didn't know you could alter the sky that much."

"Mr. Toren did it for me," Ru said. "I'm not strong enough to pull shit like that off anymore."

Ru's avatar didn't match his words. On the surface, he looked as healthy as he did at the restaurant except he wore his scar from the beginning. Evie stepped in the pool to get a better look at him. The water felt like a warm velvet caress -- and she noticed she actually felt wet this time, not only the idea of wet. It was only when she got close enough to look Ru in the eye, that she saw for herself what she already knew: Mr. Martin was not long for this world and this would be their final session.

"May I hug you?" she asked.

"Sure," Ru said, sighing with relief. "I thought you'd never ask."

They embraced.

"So," Evie asked, "what do you want to do?"

"Let's just float, if you don't mind," Ru replied. "I'm kinda tired."

"Okay. That's fine with me." Evie fell back and let the water catch her; Ru did the same. For Evie, the feeling of weightlessness was even more intense this time around.

It was as if her body just plain...evaporated. The sky was spectacular: full of oranges, pinks, and purples. The supermoon was huge, fat, and looked close enough to touch.

"Can we hold hands, Ms. Evie?" asked Ru shyly.

"Sure," Evie said. She felt for his hand and held on. At the moment it seemed to be the only solid thing.

For a long while the room was totally quiet except for their breathing. When Ru finally spoke, it startled her. "So...has school started?"

"Yeah, about a week ago, " Evie replied.

"How is it on the outside?"

"Same old crappy new normal. Right now it's hot as blazes, even though it rains cats and dogs almost every other day. My backyard looks like a rainforest. What's it like on the inside?"

"At the hospice?"

"Yeah."

"You really want to know? Cuz that shit's depressing."

She squeezed his hand. "Yeah. I want to know."

"Well, I'm down to about 110. Skin and bone. I haven't eaten in like...three days. This morning I asked them to stop giving me fluids. I come to this room a lot and just float and think, although sometimes I just float. There's no pain in here. Mr. Toren switches out skies for me."

"So...it's serious," Evie said.

"Yeah...it is. So serious I was afraid they weren't going to let me see you again."

"Are you scared?" asked Evie.

"Yeah, a little," Ru admitted. "I mean, I'm not scared of not existing. I figure it didn't hurt before I was born, so why should it hurt me when I'm gone? The devil's in the transition, though, the process of the light going out...I assume that hurts. At least a little." He fell silent, then let out a feeble laugh. "Hey, you and I can't keep from breaking the rules, can we? Because we are definitely not keeping it light. At all."

"Okay, I'll shut up and let you be," Evie offered.

Ru squeezed her hand. Even in VR, his grip was weak. "No, I don't mind. Really. I've always been a rip the bandage off kind of guy." Then, out of nowhere: "Ms. Evie, do you like cats?"

"No, I'm allergic. Why?"

"Cuz I was thinking I might come back as a cat and try and find you."

Evie just laughed. "Come back as one of those weird sea creatures that look like plants. Then all you'll have to do is sit at the bottom of the ocean and be gorgeous. And it'll be an excuse for me to get my SCUBA license."

"Nah," Ru said, "I like to move around." Then: "I wish I had time to try that one on for size, though. I'm sure Mr. Toren could arrange it."

Silence. Evie couldn't say how much time passed before Ru tried to speak again. When he finally did, it wasn't loud and it wasn't much. He whispered her name -- "Evie..." -- as a breathy prayer. Then his hand slowly faded from her grip. The clouds in the sky stopped moving -- and Evie knew she was alone.

FOURTEEN

This time the transition back to real life was smooth sailing. Evie went seamlessly from weeping in the pool to weeping in her conference room then drifting off to sleep. Forsythia pinged her early the next morning, just as she was stirring awake. Evie was tempted not to answer, but figured she'd have to deal with follow-up sometime, so she might as well take the bull by the horns. She put Forsythia on the monitor.

The digital assistant was dressed in black and greeted her with a somber expression. Was this the first patient they'd lost? "Hello, Ms. Evie. I'm just calling to check in."

"I know," Evie said wearily. "When did Mr. Martin pass?"

"One hour, ten minutes, and 37 seconds after he exited the simulation. It was very peaceful. I think he was ready."

It was all Evie could do to keep from rolling her eyes and sniping, *How would you know if he was ready or not? You're just talking lines of code.* But she restrained herself. Forsythia was doing the best she could.

"Ms. Barnes," she asked gently, "would you like to speak to the trial psychiatrist? You are scheduled for the standard study exit interviews next week, but I can arrange a conference sooner..."

"No," Evie insisted, "I'm fine." Then a stray tear proved her wrong.

"Ms. Evie," Forsythia noted, "your eyes are leaking."

Evie laughed despite herself. "Your eyes are leaking?" she repeated. "Where did you learn that one?"

"Mr. Tori says it all the time when they're about to cry. I don't think they like crying very much."

"Nobody does," said Evie. Then: "Why do you think this hurts so much? We were just strangers in the night." She knew perfectly well Forsythia only understood emotion as a data point to be parsed, but she was curious to hear her take on things.

"The simulation is completely immersive," Forsythia replied in a bright, professional tone, like she was giving a presentation. "Everything you experience in it is, for all practical purposes, real. So if you made a connection in VR, it felt as immediate as if Mr. Martin had been physically present."

"So it's only logical, yes?"

"Yes -- but I know my response is inadequate to your pain."

FIFTEEN

Evie stumbled through the next week under a pall of gray. Days were spent in her conference room teaching; evenings were spent in exit interviews and grading homework.

Then on Saturday morning she got a surprise. She and Ms. Vicki were chatting over breakfast (the almost nightly happy hours had stopped with the start of school) when Vicki suddenly said: "Evie girl, don't look now, but one of those super expensive putt-putt cars that run on air and magic just pulled into your driveway."

Evie grabbed her phone, ran to the living room, kneeled on the sofa, and peered through her blinds. Sure enough, there was a silver Aston 385D parked in her driveway looking like a shimmery metallic insect from outer space.

"So who's in the car?" Vicki pestered.

"Don't know. It's just sitting there at the moment. No one's gotten out yet and the windows are tinted."

"Ooooo, I love it! A mystery!"

Eventually the driver's side door popped upwards like a ladybug's wing. Someone dressed head to toe in flowing cream hazard wear unfolded themselves out of the tiny vehicle. They looked like a high tech desert nomad. They stretched, then started up the short walkway to her steps.

"Gotta go!" Evie said and disconnected. She scrambled off the sofa and grabbed the mask she kept by the door. She held her breath as the cream colored ghost glided up the stairs and rang her bell. *Oh my god,* Evie thought with envy, *that outfit is stunning! I wonder how much that gear costs.*

"Good morning," they said over the intercom. "Is this the Barnes residence?" They had a masculine sounding voice, deep, but not too deep, and strangely familiar.

"Why yes, it is." Evie unlatched and opened the main door, but kept the glass storm door locked just in case. Even though her unexpected visitor was totally covered in creamy silk like fabric except for their eyes, she knew exactly who it was. The soulful light brown eyes gave them away, and those eyes were ten times more intense in real life than they were in VR. "Toren McDonald?"

"Yes, Evelyn, it's me," they replied. "I apologize for showing up unannounced, but I was in the area. May I come in?"

She unlatched the storm door. "Sure, come in."

"Thank you, Ms. Barnes."

They crossed the threshold into her living room. The first thing Evie was struck by was their height. She already knew Toren had a good eight inches on her, but somehow in VR -- even with all the upgrades -- the height difference didn't seem as pronounced as it did then. She tried to picture Toren as a child: the tallest in their class by a head, orphaned and grappling with gender issues, with a lightning quick mind that could reach the stars. It wasn't a recipe for happiness. She didn't envy their childhood one bit.

"Do you mind if I remove my gloves?" they asked.

"Not at all," she replied. "Just place them in the sanitizer over there. They'll be clean in five minutes."

When Toren dropped their hood back, Evie got another shock. Toren had dreads, and judging from the length she could see, they'd had them for a while.

"Your hair..." she said. "It's...long."

Evie couldn't see the bottom half of their face, but judging from the twinkle in their eyes and the laugh lines, she knew they were smiling. "Yes, my professional avatar is not completely true as far as the hair is concerned. That allows me some privacy in the real world. Few people know what my hair really looks like. I do like custom suits, though."

Evie gestured towards the sofa. "Have a seat. Could I get you something to drink?"

"No, thank you," they replied.

Evie sat in the other chair. "So what brings you out to the real world, Toren?"

"I wanted to see how you were doing," they replied. "Your time with Mr. Martin was shorter and more intense than I expected. I thought you would have a couple months together at least."

Evie shrugged. "The best laid plans of mice and men..."

"How are you holding up?" Toren asked.

"I'm fine," Evie replied. "Although I think about Ru a lot for someone I barely knew. I wish I'd gotten to meet him earlier. We could have been friends." She smiled to herself, then added: "And maybe more."

"Would you like me to arrange additional meetings with the psychiatrist?"

"No," Evie assured them. "Seriously, I'm fine. It hurts, yeah, but it's supposed to hurt."

"What do you mean?"

"Not everything in life is supposed to feel good," Evie replied. "And I can deal with that. You can't avoid the hard stuff. But, I'll have to say: until your trial, I always thought of VR as primarily make-believe -- but now I realize it can be as real as you let it."

Silence. Toren fished a small box from the folds of their flowing garment and placed it on the coffee table. "Mr. Martin wanted you to have this. It's his dog tags. Usually, they're buried with the soldier or given to next of kin, but since Ru didn't have any we can find, he wanted you to have them."

Evie eyed the box on the table, but refrained from taking a look inside. She wasn't ready. She also didn't want Toren to see her with her eyes leaking. "May I ask you a question?" she asked.

"Sure."

"Did you know before the study the military stole the code for *Hololounge*?"

"I suspected as much," Toren replied. "Although I didn't know what they did with it until Mr. Martin told me what happened to him."

"That was awful what they did," Evie said.

"Yes, it was," Toren agreed. "And what's worse is that I'm partially responsible."

Well. Evie wasn't going to argue with them there. "Did you know what happened to Ru before you paired us together?"

"No," Toren replied. "Mr. Martin didn't tell me until after he had told you. You listened to him, Evelyn. And by doing that, you gave him a great gift; you allowed him peace... Which brings me to the other reason I've come here today..."

Evie's stomach tightened. What more could they possibly want from her?

Toren continued: "In a few months, we will be doing another test of the system at a children's hospital. I'd like you to participate. It will be a similar situation. Terminal children without family. That happens more often than you think these days."

"Yeah," Evie said, "at a certain time in your life, it could have happened to you."

Toren's eyes widened. Obviously it hadn't occurred to them Evie knew anything about their past.

"Don't think I didn't look you up before I met with you," Evie went on. "There's not much of your personal info on the net -- I gather you work hard to limit it -- but I do know you lived in an orphanage and were in foster care for a while before that professor discovered you."

"But I didn't design my system primarily with myself in mind," Toren revealed. "I designed it in memory of my oldest daughter who perished in the second wave. She, of course, had a loving family, but we still couldn't be there with her. She died alone without us. Her little sister was positively heartbroken -- I mean, we all were -- but I think she was most of all. It took her a long time for her to understand why her big sister was never coming home."

Evie felt like she'd been punched in the stomach. She couldn't imagine what it would be like to lose a child. She only knew she'd be devastated if she lost a student to the plagues. Thankfully, by the grace of the universe, she'd been spared that heartache so far. "Oh Toren, I'm so sorry. I didn't know."

"The pain ebbs and swells," they said wistfully, "but it is always with me. At least you'll understand now that designing this system has primarily been a labor of love."

"Well, I don't know if I can participate in your next test..." Evie said. "I mean, I've got my classes..."

"There is no rush. You have a few months to make a decision," Toren said. "But based on your teaching experience, as well as the quality of your interaction with Mr. Martin, I'd think you'd be ideal."

Silence. Evie stared at her hands.

"I have another proposal too," Toren announced, "and this one might be more to your liking..."

Oh god what now? Evie thought.

"After *Hololounge* won the contest," Toren began, "Mederra read the book..."

Evie was astounded. She assumed Mederra was Toren's wife and if Evie's memory served her correctly, it was the first time Toren had mentioned their wife's name in her presence. Huh. That must mean Toren was beginning to trust her. "What did she think?"

Toren chuckled at the memory. "She thought it was crap. Same as you. But she welcomed the infusion of prize money into our then meager bank account. When I explained to her that there were real rooms similar to the *Hololounge* simulation I'd constructed, do you know what her reaction was?"

"I don't know. What?"

"*What a spectacular waste of imagination!* While she could understand the impulse to create a nostalgic fantasy to relieve some of the stress of the pandemic, she also believed that in the end it was self-destructive and wasteful. Why only wistfully dream of the past? Why not spend all that nervous energy dreaming up a new future?"

"Think about it," Toren continued. "Everything we've done -- all the research, all the innovation, all the protests, all the vitriol -- has been to reach some kind of stability so we can ultimately drift back to a slightly improved version of what we did before. With a few notable exceptions, there are very few people who really want radical change. But our *before was* unsustainable; *before* is what got us to where we are today. We almost need to start from scratch, but we need a safe place to experiment, to play, to try new worlds on for size, a laboratory if you will."

Evie shrugged. "No argument there. So how would your wife remedy that situation?"

Toren produced another object from their garment and placed it on the coffee table next to the box that contained Rupert Martin's dog tags. It was a tiny goldtone flash drive shaped like an antique key. "For the past year, we've been hosting a variant of *Hololounge* using the same VR and augmented reality system that you used with Mr. Martin -- except we don't attempt to recreate a past we can never recover; we dream the future."

"How the hell do you dream the future?" Evie asked laughing.

Toren laughed too. "I know I sound ridiculous."

"Yeah you do."

"It's the same rules as those in the book. You construct a character and go about your day. Where do you work? What is work? How do you dress? Are you in love? Do you have children? Where do they go to school? What is school? It's all up for grabs. Keep it light. Use your imagination. Have fun."

"How many people are doing this?" asked Evie.

"100 at last count. From 15 countries and 3 continents," Toren replied.

"Are they all like you?"

"What do you mean?"

"Are they all wealthy?"

"No," Toren replied. "Mederra and I made certain of that. Why repeat the mistakes of the past?"

"What's the key for?" asked Evie, pointing to the flash drive on the coffee table.

"It's your passport to the game. I'm inviting you. Insert that into your main console and you'll gain access to a tutorial and further instructions. We meet on the second and fourth Tuesdays each month. You're welcome to lurk until you get a feel for things."

"Why me?" Evie asked.

"Because you have a healthy sense of adventure. And I suspect you'll enjoy it. I know I do. It gives me hope when my supply runs low. Players are extremely resourceful and creative."

Evie picked up the flash drive and examined it. Who would have guessed a random text during breakfast would eventually lead to an invitation to an exclusive multiplayer VR game where folks from all over the world attempted to dream the future? That certainly wasn't on her bingo card. But then again: none of this was.

Toren covered their head again and stood. Their visit was almost over. "You don't have to decide right now. But do think about it. I, for one, would love to have you, even though when you enter the game, I won't know who you are."

Evie wished they wouldn't go. They were just beginning to open up; they were just getting interesting. "Are you sure you don't want something to eat or drink?" she offered again. "I can whip something up. No problem."

"No, but thank you kindly for your hospitality," Toren replied. They grabbed their gloves from the sanitizer and put them on.

Evie unlatched the doors. "Goodbye, Toren -- and be well. Thanks for checking up on me. It was very kind of you. And: you've certainly given me plenty to think about."

Their eyes twinkled. "I aim to please," they said as they crossed the threshold. "Hopefully, we'll meet again."

Evie watched Toren glide down her front steps. Then, she closed the door and ran to the sofa so she could watch them drive away.

Evie had put the key into her pocket, but as soon as Toren was gone, she took it out to stare at it again. She checked the calendar on her watch only to discover that the fourth Tuesday, which is when the game would meet next, was just over a week away. That seemed like forever, but she had no choice but to wait. Still, she was buzzing with excitement and she had to put that energy somewhere. So she grabbed her phone from the coffee table and dialed Vicki's number.

"Girl," she said, "you wouldn't believe who just left."

ABOUT THE AUTHOR

FRANETTA MCMILLIAN has been writing ever since her mother taught her how to hold a pencil. Her writing and artwork have been featured in *Dreamstreets, Gargoyle, The Broadkill Review, H2SO4,* as well as other print and online publications. She also publishes the zine *Fat Black Girl in a Wheelchair*. She splits her time between Avondale, PA, and Newark, DE, crossing the border only at night.